CAVE BIRDS

CAVE BIRDS

An Alchemical Cave Drama

Poems by Ted Hughes and

drawings by Leonard Baskin

The Viking Press · New York

Text Copyright © Ted Hughes, 1978
Illustrations Copyright in all countries
of the International Copyright Union
by Leonard Baskin, 1978
Published in 1978 by The Viking Press
625 Madison Avenue, New York, N.Y. 10022

Library of Congress Cataloging in Publication Data:
Hughes, Ted, 1930–
Cave birds
I. Baskin, Leonard, 1922–
PR6058.U37C33   821'.9'14   78–6662

ISBN 0–670–20927–9

Printed in Great Britain

CONTENTS

To
ERIC WALTER WHITE

The scream

There was the sun on the wall — my childhood's
Nursery picture. And there was my gravestone
Which shared my dreams, and ate and drank with me happily.

All day the hawk perfected its craftsmanship
And even through the night the miracle persisted.

Mountains lazed in their smoky camp.
Worms in the ground were doing a good job.

Flesh of bronze, stirred with a bronze thirst,
Like a newborn baby at the breast,
Slept in the sun's mercy.

And the inane weights of iron
That come suddenly crashing into people, out of nowhere,
Only made me feel brave and creaturely.

When I saw little rabbits with their heads crushed on roads
I knew I rode the wheel of the galaxy.

Calves' heads all dew-bristled with blood on counters
Grinned like masks, and sun and moon danced.

And my mate with his face sewn up
Where they'd opened it to take something out
Raised a hand —

He smiled, in half-coma,
A stone temple smile.

Then I, too, opened my mouth to praise —

But a silence wedged my gullet.

Like an obsidian dagger, dry, jag-edged,
A silent lump of volcanic glass,

The scream
Vomited itself.

The summoner

Spectral, gigantified,
Protozoic, blood-eating.

The carapace
Of foreclosure.

The cuticle
Of final arrest.

Among crinkling of oak-leaves — an effulgence,
Occasionally glimpsed.

Shadow stark on the wall, all night long,
From the street-light. A sigh.

Evidence, rinds and empties,
That he also ate here.

Before dawn, your soul, sliding back,
Beholds his bronze image, grotesque on the bed.

You grow to recognise the identity
Of your protector.

Sooner or later —
The grip.

After the first fright

I sat up and took stock of my options.
I argued my way out of every thought anybody could think
But not out of the stopping and starting
Catherine wheel in my belly.
The disputation went beyond me too quickly.
When I said : 'Civilisation,'
He began to chop off his fingers and mourn.
When I said : 'Sanity and again Sanity and above all Sanity,'
He disembowelled himself with a cross-shaped cut.
I stopped trying to say anything.
But then when he began to snore in his death-struggle
The guilt came.
And when they covered his face I went cold.

The interrogator

Small hope now for the stare-boned mule of man
Lumped on the badlands, at his concrete shadow.

This bird is the sun's key-hole.
The sun spies through her. Through her

He ransacks the camouflage of hunger.

Investigation
By grapnel.

Some angered righteous questions
Agitate her craw.

The blood-louse
Of ether.

With her prehensile goad of interrogation
Her eye on the probe

Her olfactory x-ray
She ruffles the light that chills the startled eyeball.

After, a dripping bagful of evidence
Under her humped robe,

She sweeps back, a spread-fingered Efreet,
Into the courts of the after-life.

She seemed so considerate

And everything had become so hideous
My solemn friends sat twice as solemn
My jokey friends joked and joked

But their heads sweated decay, like dead things I'd left in a bag
And had forgotten to get rid of.

I bit the back of my hand
And sniffed mortification.

Then the bird came.
She said: your world has died.
It sounded dramatic.
But my pet fern, the one fellow creature I still cherished,
It actually had died.
I felt life had decided to cancel me
As if it saw better hope for itself elsewhere.

Then this bird-being embraced me, saying:
'Look up at the sun. I am the one creature
Who never harmed any living thing.'

I was glad to shut my eyes, and be held.
Whether dead or unborn, I did not care.

The judge

The pondering body of the law teeters across
A web-glistening geometry.

Lolling, he receives and transmits
Cosmic equipoise.

The garbage-sack of everything that is not
The Absolute onto whose throne he lowers his buttocks.

Clowning, half-imbecile,
A Nero of the unalterable.

His gluttony
Is a strange one — his leavings are guilt and sentence.

Hung with precedents as with obsolete armour
His banqueting court is as airy as any idea.

At all hours he comes wobbling out
To fatten on the substance of those who have fouled

His tarred and starry web.

Or squats listening
To his digestion and the solar silence.

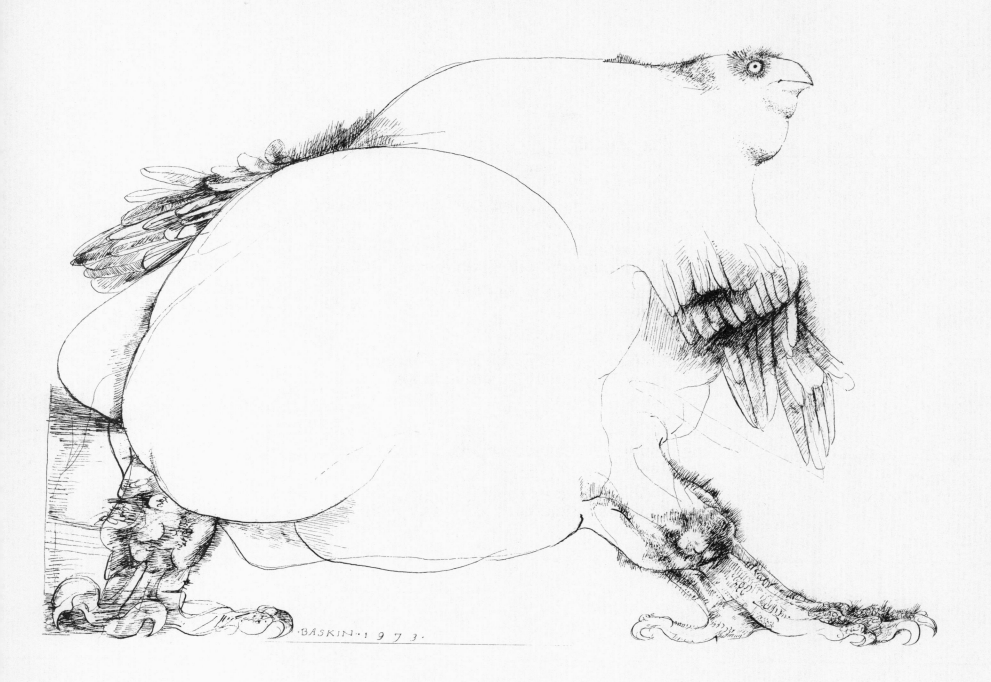

BASKIN · 1 9 7 3 ·

The plaintiff

This is the bird of light!

This is your moon of pain — and the wise night-bird
Your smile's shadow.

This bird
Is the life-divining bush of your desert

The heavy-fruited, burning tree
Of your darkness.

How you have nursed her!

Her feathers are leaves, the leaves tongues,
The mouths wounds, the tongues flames

The feet
Roots

Buried in your chest, a humbling weight
That will not let you breathe.

Your heart's winged flower
Come to supplant you.

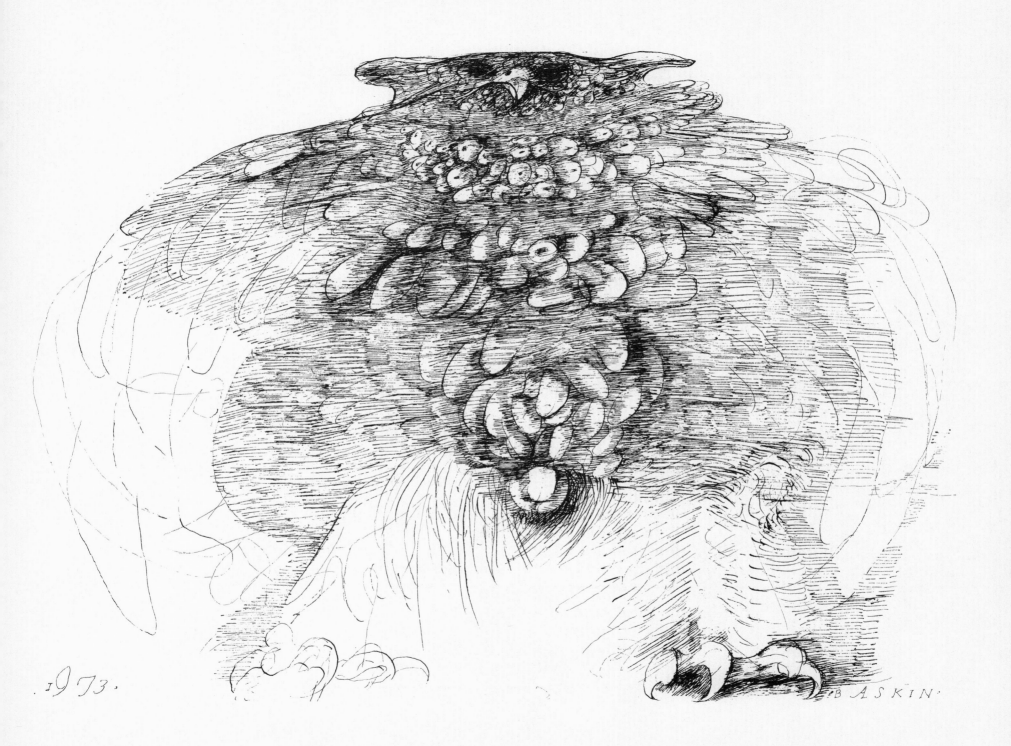

In these fading moments I wanted to say

How close I come to a flame
Just watching sticky flies play

How I cry unspeakable outcry
Reading the newspaper that smells of stale refuse

How I just let the excess delight
Spill out of my eyes, as I walk along

How imbecile innocent I am

So some perfect stranger's maiming
Numbs me in freezing petroleum
And lights it, and lets me char to the spine

Even the dead sparrow's eye
Lifts the head off me — like a chloroform

But she was murmuring: Right from the start, my life
Has been a cold business of mountains and their snow
Of rivers and their mud

Yes there were always smiles and one will do a lot
To be near one's friends

But after the bye-byes, and even before the door closed, even while the lips
    still moved
The scree had not ceased to slip and trickle
The snow-melt was cutting deeper
Through its anaesthetic
The brown bulging swirls, where the snowflakes vanished into themselves
Had lost every reflection.

The whole earth
Had turned in its bed
To the wall.

20

The executioner

Fills up
Sun, moon, stars, he fills them up

With his hemlock —
They darken

He fills up the evening and the morning, they darken
He fills up the sea

He comes in under the blind filled-up heaven
Across the lightless filled-up face of water

He fills up the rivers he fills up the roads, like tentacles
He fills up the streams and the paths, like veins

The tap drips darkness darkness
Sticks to the soles of your feet

He fills up the mirror, he fills up the cup
He fills up your thoughts to the brims of your eyes

You just see he is filling the eyes of your friends
And now lifting your hand you touch at your eyes

Which he has completely filled up
You touch him

You have no idea what has happened
To what is no longer yours

It feels like the world
Before your eyes ever opened

22

·BASKIN· 1973·

The accused

Confesses his body —
The gripful of daggers.

And confesses his skin — the bedaubed, begauded
Eagle-dancer.

His heart —
The soul-stuffed despot.

His stomach —
The corpse-eating god.

And his hard life-lust — the blind
Swan of insemination.

And his hard brain — the sacred assassin.

On a flame-horned mountain-stone, in the sun's disc,
He heaps them all up, for the judgment.

So there his atoms are annealed, as in x-rays,
Of their blood-aberration —

His mudded body, lord of middens, like an ore,

To rainbowed clinker and a beatitude.

First, the doubtful charts of skin

Came into my hands — I set out.

After some harmless, irrelevant marvels
And much boredom at sea

Came the wrecked landfall, sharp rocks, hands and knees
Then the small and large intestine, in their wet cave.
These gave me pause.

Then came the web of veins
Where I hung so long
For the giant spider's pleasure, twitching in the darkest corner.

Finally
After the skull-hill of visions and the battle in the valley of screams

After the islands of women

I came to loose bones
On a heathery moor, and a roofless church.

Wild horses, with blowing tails and manes,
Standing among graves.

And a leaning menhir, with my name on it.
And an epitaph, which read:
'Under this rock, he found weapons.'

The knight

Has conquered. He has surrendered everything.

Now he kneels. He is offering up his victory
And unlacing his steel.

In front of him are the common wild stones of the earth —

The first and last altar
Onto which he lowers his spoils.

And that is right. He has conquered in earth's name.
Committing these trophies

To the small madness of roots, to the mineral stasis
And to rain.

An unearthly cry goes up.
The Universes squabble over him —

Here a bone, there a rag.
His sacrifice is perfect. He reserves nothing.

Skylines tug him apart, winds drink him,
Earth itself unravels him from beneath —

His submission is flawless.

Blueflies lift off his beauty.
Beetles and ants officiate

Pestering him with instructions.
His patience grows only more vast.

His eyes darken bolder in their vigil
As the chapel crumbles.

His spine survives its religion,
The texts moulder —

The quaint courtly language
Of wingbones and talons.

And already
Nothing remains of the warrior but his weapons

And his gaze.
Blades, shafts, unstrung bows — and the skull's beauty

Wrapped in the rags of his banner.
He is himself his banner and its rags.

While hour by hour the sun
Strengthens its revelation.

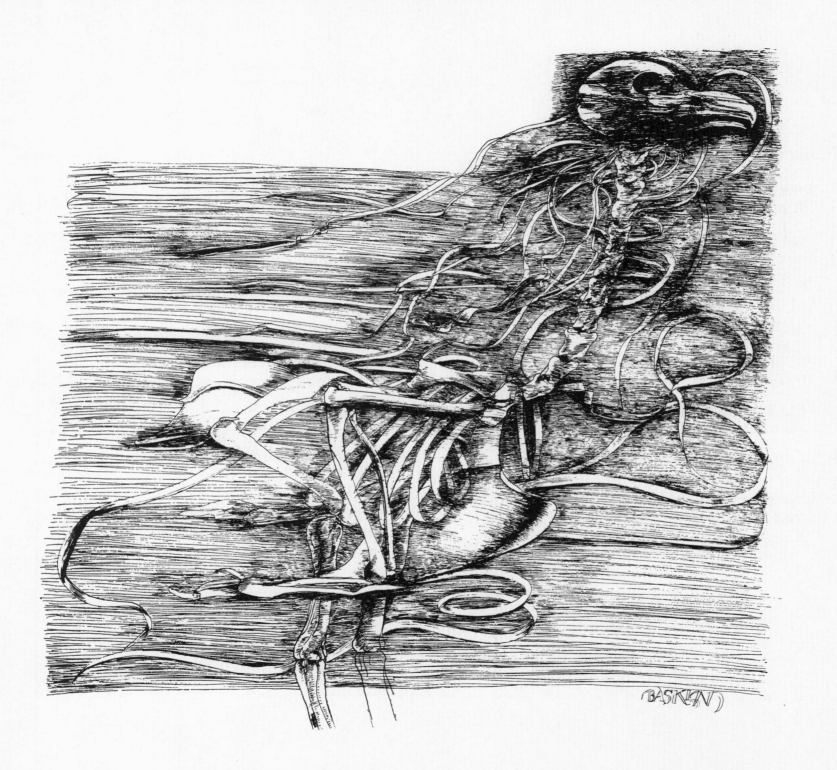

Something was happening

While I strolled
Where a leaf or two still tapped like bluetits

I met thin, webby rain
And thought: 'Ought I to turn back, or keep going?'
Her heart stopped beating, that second.

As I hung up my coat and went through into the kitchen
And peeled a flake off the turkey's hulk,
                     and stood vacantly munching
Her sister got the call from the hospital
And gasped out the screech.

And all the time
I was scrubbing at my nails and staring
                        through the window
She was burning.

Some, who had been close, walked away
Because it was beyond help now.

They did not stay to watch
Her body trying to sit up, her face unrecognisable
As she tried to tell
How it went on getting worse and worse
Till she sank back.

And when I saw new emerald tufting the quince, in April
And cried in dismay: 'Here it comes again!'
The leather of my shoes
Continued to gleam
The silence of the furniture
Registered nothing

The earth, right to its far rims, ignored me.

Only the eagle-hunter
Beating himself to keep warm
And bowing towards his trap
Started singing

(Two, three, four thousand years off key.)

30

''1975'' GASKIN

The gatekeeper

A sphynx.
A two-headed questioner.

First, a question —
The simple fork in the road.

You choose — but it is a formality.
Already yourself has confessed yourself.

All those sweatings and grinnings are futile.
The candidate is stripped.

Such fear — your weight oozes from you.
No matter, it was upholstering ease,

It was insulation
From this stranger who wails out your name

Then drops, hugging a bare piece of ground
Where everything is too late.

Remorse, promises, a monkey chatter
Blurting from every orifice.

Your cry is like a gasp from a corpse.
Everything comes back. And a wingspread

Nails you with its claws. And an eagle
Is flying

To drop you into a bog or carry you to eagles.

A flayed crow in the hall of judgment

Darkness has all come together, making an egg.
Darkness in which there is now nothing.

A blot has knocked me down. It clogs me.
A globe of blot, a drop of unbeing.

Nothingness came close and breathed on me — a frost
A shawl of annihilation has curled me up like a new foetus.

I rise beyond height — I fall past falling.
I float on an air
As mist-balls float, and as stars.

A condensation, a gleam simplification
Of all that pertained.
This cry alone struggled in its tissues.

Where am I going? What will come to me here?
Is this everlasting? Is it
Stoppage and the start of nothing?

Or am I under attention?
Do purposeful cares incubate me?
Am I the self of some spore

In this white of death blackness,
This yoke of afterlife?
What feathers shall I have? What is my weakness good for?

A great fear rests
On the thing I am, as a feather on a hand.

I shall not fight
Against whatever is allotted to me.

My soul skinned, and the soul-skin laid out
A mat for my judges.

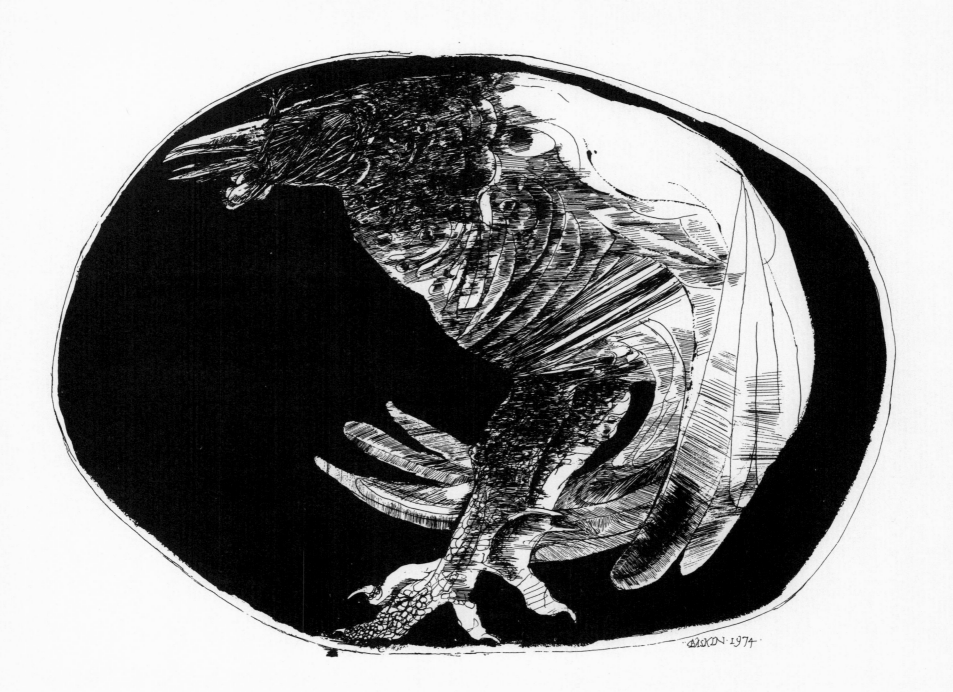

The baptist

Enfolds you
In winding waters, a swathing of balm

A mummy bandaging
Of all your body's puckering hurts

In the circulation of sea.
A whale of furtherance

Cruises through the Arctic of stone,
Carrying you blindfold and gagged.

You dissolve, in the cool wholesome salts
Like a hard-cornered grief, drop by drop

Or an iceberg of loss
Shrinking towards the equator

Or a seed in its armour.

Baskin 1974.

Only a little sleep, a little slumber

And suddenly you
Have not a word to say for yourself.

Only a little knife, a small incision,
A snickety nick in the brain
And you drop off, like a polyp.

Only a crumb of fungus,
A pulp of mouldy tinder
And you flare, fluttering, black-out like a firework.

Who are you, in the nest among the bones?
You are the shyest bird among birds.

'I am the last of my kind.'

A green mother

Why are you afraid?
In the house of the dead are many cradles.
The earth is a busy hive of heavens.
This is one lottery that cannot be lost.

Here is the heaven of the tree:
Angels will come to collect you.
And here are the heavens of the flowers:
These are an everliving bliss, a pulsing, a bliss in sleep.

And here is the heaven of the worm —
A forgiving God.
Little of you will be rejected —
Which the angels of the flowers will gladly collect.

And here is the heaven of insects.
From all these you may climb
To the heavens of the birds,
          the heavens of the beasts, and of the fish.

These are only some heavens
Not all within your choice.
There are also the heavens
Of your persuasion.
Your candle prayers have congealed an angel, a star.

The city of religions
Is like a city of hotels, a holiday city.
I am your guide.
In none of these is the aftertaste of death
Pronounced poor. This earth is heaven's sweetness.

It is heaven's mother.
The grave is her breast
And her milk is endless life.
                          You shall see
How tenderly she has wiped her child's face clean

Of the bitumen of blood and the smoke of tears.

As I came, I saw a wood

Where trees stood in dirt, clutching at the sky
Like savages photographed in the middle of a ritual
Birds danced among them and animals took part
Insects too and around their feet flowers

And time was not present they never stopped
Or left anything old or reached any new thing
Everything moved in an excitement that seemed permanent

They were so ecstatic
I could go in among them, touch them, even break pieces off them
Pluck up flowers, without disturbing them in the least.
The birds simply flew wide, but were not for one moment distracted
From the performance of their feathers and eyes.
And the animals the same, though they avoided me
They did so with holy steps and never paused
In the glow of fur which was their absolution in sanctity

And their obedience, I could see that.

I could see I stood in a paradise of tremblings

At the crowded crossroads of all the heavens
The festival of all the religions

But a voice, a bell of cracked iron
Jarred in my skull

Summoning me to prayer

To eat flesh and to drink blood.

1976.

Baskin

A riddle

Who am I?

Just as you are my father
I am your bride.

As your speech sharpened
My silence widened.

As your laughter fitted itself
My dumbness stretched its mouth wider

As you chose your direction
I was torn up and dragged

As you defended yourself
I collected your blows, I was knocked backward

As you dodged
I received in full

As you attacked
I was beneath your feet

As you saved yourself
I was lost

When you arrived empty
I gathered up all you had and forsook you

Now as you face your death
I offer you your life

Just as surely as you are my father
I shall deliver you

My firstborn
Into a changed, unchangeable world
Of wind and of sun, of rock and water
To cry.

The scapegoat

The beautiful thing beckoned, big-haunched he loped,
Swagged with wealth, full-organed he tottered,

His sweetnesses dribbled,
His fever misted, he wanted to sob,

His cry starved watering,
Shudderings bone-juddered his hot weakness.

The frilled lizard of cavort
Ran in his wheel like a man, burned by breath.

The baboon of panoply
Jumped at the sky-rump of a greasy rainbow.

The flag of the crotch, his glistenings tapered to touch,
Furled and unfurled, in chill draughts of sun.

The comedian
Of the leap out of the body and back in again

Let out a mandrake shriek
In a jabber of unborn spirits, a huddle of oracles.

The joker
That the confederate pack has to defer to

Gambled and lost the whole body —
An I.O.U. signed by posterity, a smear on the light.

The champion of the swoon
Lolled his bauble head, a puppet, a zombie

And the lord of immortality is a carcase of opals,
A wine-skin of riddance, a goat of oaths

A slaking of thistles.

After there was nothing there was a woman

Whose face had reached her mirror
Via the vulture's gullet
And the droppings of the wild dog, and she remembers it
Massaging her brow with cream

Whose breasts had come about
By long toil of earthworms
After many failures, but they were here now
And she protected them with silk

Her bones
Lay as they did because they could not escape anything
They hung as it were in space
The targets of every bombardment

She had found her belly
In a clockwork pool, wound by the winding and unwinding sea.
First it was her toy, then she found its use
And curtained it with a flowered skirt.
It made her eyes shine.

She looked at the grass trembling among the worn stones

Having about as much comprehension as a lamb
Who stares around at everything simultaneously
With ant-like head and soldierly bearing

She had made it but only just, just —

Baskin
19.76

The guide

When everything that can fall has fallen
Something rises.
And leaving here, and evading there
And that, and this, is my headway.

Where the snow glare blinded you
I start.
Where the snow mama cuddled you warm
I fly up. I lift you.

Tumbling worlds
Open my way

And you cling.

And we go

Into the wind. The flame-wind — a red wind
And a black wind. The red wind comes
To empty you. And the black wind, the longest wind
The headwind

To scour you.

Then the non-wind, a least breath,
Fills you from easy sources.

I am the needle

Magnetic
A tremor

The searcher
The finder

His legs ran about

Till they tangled and seemed to trip and lie down
With her legs intending to hold them there forever

His arms lifted things, groped in dark rooms, at last with their hands
Caught her arms
And lay down enwoven at last at last

Mouth talked its way in and out and finally
Found her mouth and settled deeper deeper

His chest pushed until it came up against
Her breast at the end of everything

His navel fitted over her navel as closely as possible
Like a mirror face down flat on a mirror

And so when every part
Like a bull pushing towards its cows, not to be stayed
Like a calf seeking its mama
Like a desert staggerer, among his hallucinations
Seeking the hoof-churned hole

Finally got what it needed, and grew still, and closed its eyes

Then such greatness and truth descended

As over a new grave, when the mourners have gone
And the stars come out
And the earth, bristling and raw, tiny and lost,
Resumes its search

Rushing through the vast astonishment.

Walking bare

What is left is just what my life bought me
The gem of myself.
A bare certainty, without confection.
Through this blowtorch light little enough

But enough.
The stones do not cease to support me.
Valleys unfold their invitations.
A progress beyond assay, breath by breath.

I rest just at my weight.
Movement is still patient with me —
Lightness beyond lightness releasing me further.

And the mountains of torment and mica
Pass me by.

And new skylines lift wider wings
Of simpler light.

The blood wrapped cries have hardened
To moisteners for my mouth.

Hurrying worlds of voices, on other errands,
Traffic through me, ignore me.

A one gravity keeps touching me.

For I am the appointed planet
Extinct in an emptiness

But a spark in the breath
Of the corolla that sweeps me.

Bride and groom lie hidden for three days

She gives him his eyes, she found them
Among some rubble, among some beetles

He gives her her skin
He just seemed to pull it down out of the air
                              and lay it over her
She weeps with fearfulness and astonishment

She has found his hands for him,
                    and fitted them freshly at the wrists
They are amazed at themselves,
                        they go feeling all over her

He has assembled her spine,
                    he cleaned each piece carefully
And sets them in perfect order
A superhuman puzzle but he is inspired
She leans back twisting this way and that,
                    using it and laughing incredulously

Now she has brought his feet, she is connecting them
So that his whole body lights up

And he has fashioned her new hips
With all fittings complete and with newly wound coils,
                        all shiningly oiled
He is polishing every part,
                    he himself can hardly believe it

They keep taking each other to the sun,
                        they find they can easily
To test each new thing at each new step
And now she smooths over him the plates of his skull
So that the joints are invisible
And now he connects her throat,
                    her breasts and the pit of her stomach
With a single wire

She gives him his teeth, tying their roots
                        to the centrepin of his body

He sets the little circlets on her fingertips
She stitches his body here and there
                        with steely purple silk
He oils the delicate cogs of her mouth
She inlays with deep-cut scrolls the nape of his neck
He sinks into place the inside of her thighs

So, gasping with joy, with cries of wonderment
Like two gods of mud
Sprawling in the dirt, but with infinite care

They bring each other to perfection.

56

1976   ·BASKIN·

The owl flower

Big terror descends.

A drumming glare, a flickering face of flames.

Something separates into a signal,
Plaintive, a filament of incandescence,

As it were a hair.

In the maelstrom's eye,
In the core of the brimming heaven-blossom,
Under the tightening whorl of plumes, a mote
Scalds in dews.

A leaf of the earth
Applies to it, a cooling health.

A coffin spins in the torque.
Wounds flush with sap, headful of pollen,
Wet with nectar
The dead one stirs.

A mummy grain is cracking its smile
In the cauldron of tongues.

The ship of flowers
Nudges the wharf of skin.

The egg-stone
Bursts among broody petals —

And a staggering thing
Fired with rainbows, raw with cringing heat,

Blinks at the source.

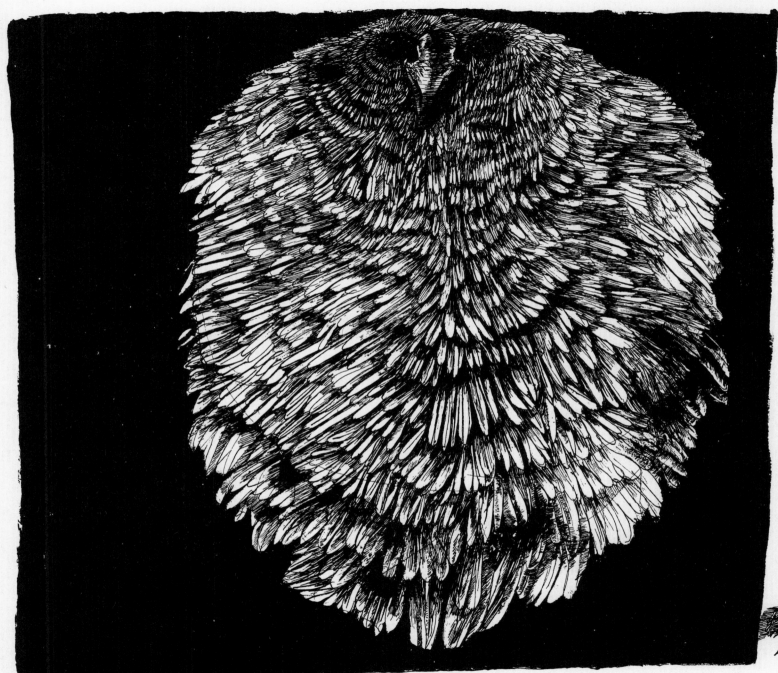

1974

The risen

He stands, filling the doorway
In the shell of earth.

He lifts wings, he leaves the remains of something,
A mess of offal, muddled as an afterbirth.

His each wingbeat — a convict's release.
What he carries will be plenty.

He slips behind the world's brow
As music escapes its skull, its clock and its skyline.

Under his sudden shadow, flames cry out among thickets.
When he soars, his shape

Is a cross, eaten by light,
On the Creator's face.

He shifts world weirdly as sunspots
Emerge as earthquakes.

A burning unconsumed,
A whirling tree —

Where he alights
A skin sloughs from a leafless apocalypse.

On his lens
Each atom engraves with a diamond.

In the wind-fondled crucible of his splendour
The dirt becomes God.

But when will he land
On a man's wrist.

Finale

At the end of the ritual
                          up comes a goblin.